The Halloween Showdown

by Eileen Ross   illustrated by Lynn Rowe Reed

Holiday House • New York

Grandmother Katt sat nestled among the cornstalks, sewing the final touches on her granddaughter's Halloween costume. "Come take a look," she called to Tabithia, who frolicked in the nearby pumpkin and squash. But before Tabithia could reply, out of the North, there came a horrendous screech.

N

E

S

Grandmother struggled to her feet, yelling, "Run, Tabithia, run! It's Grizzorka the Witch!" She hobbled toward the edge of the garden as fast as her old arthritic legs could carry her. But prickled old Grizzorka had already swooped down and captured Tabithia. "Don't worry," shouted Grandmother. "I'll save you."

"Why, you're nothing but a feeble old granny cat," cackled Grizzorka, clutching Tabithia as she flew through the trees. "You'll save nothing but your breath, and I have a new Halloween cat."

At that moment, Grandmother declared war—
war on Grizzorka the Witch!

She stripped the garden scarecrow of his faded
jacket and quickly dressed for battle. The sleeves
were a bit long, but she managed to fasten all
the brass buttons, except, of course, for the one
that was missing.

Next, she split a round orange pumpkin. She scooped
out the seeds, then cut two ear holes in one of
the halves. She placed the pumpkin helmet on her
head and made a fat kettledrum with the other half.
Grandmother thought that soldiers heading off
to war should always carry drums to hammer out
a marching beat.

Finally, she fashioned a spear out of cornstalks.
She armed the spear with her sharp sewing needle,
then headed North, banging the drum as she went.

THUB, THUB, THUB-A-DUB, DUB.

Grandmother soon met a hairy-legged spider perched high in the crook of a tree. "Where to, Old Puss?" asked Spider.

"I'm off to make war on Grizzorka the Witch, for she has stolen my darling kit."

Spider slid down the tree, her silver thread, an anchoring rope. "Grizzorka is a thief who steals my beautiful webs — especially at Halloween. I'll help you make war on the witch."

So Grandmother and Spider marched North, banging the drum as they went.

THUB, THUB, THUB-A-DUB, DUB.

Presently, they came to a pond. "Where to, Old Puss?" asked Frog, who had dug himself into the mud.

"I'm off to make war on Grizzorka the Witch, for she has stolen my darling kit."

Frog hauled himself out of the mud. "Grizzorka kidnapped my seven brothers and twelve sisters to simmer in her Halloween stew. I'll help you make war on the witch."

So Grandmother, Spider, and Frog marched North, banging the drum as they went.

THUB, THUB, THUB-A-DUB, DUB.

Soon they arrived at the
edge of Grizzorka's woods.
A sudden flap of wings caused
them all to jump and scatter.

"Who goes there?" asked a
furry black bat hanging upside
down in a tree. After proper
introductions were made, Bat
asked, "Where to, Old Puss?"

**"I'm off to make war
on Grizzorka the Witch,
for she has stolen
my darling kit."**

Bat stretched his wings.
"Grizzorka teaches everyone
to be afraid of bats even
though we keep insects from
becoming a nuisance. That
nasty old crone has ruined my
reputation. I'll help you make
war on the witch."

"Come along, then," said Grandmother, "but be quiet. Grizzorka's house is nearby." They all sneaked through the forest so Grizzorka wouldn't hear them coming.

THUB, THUB, THUB-A-DUB, DUB.

Now, Grandmother didn't want the witch to know how large her army had become, so one by one, she ushered Spider, Frog, and Bat into the pockets of her jacket. Then she tiptoed toward Grizzorka's tumbledown hut.

As she peeked in through the window, her nose began to twitch. Apparently, the witch had sprinkled too much pepper in the Halloween stew. Grandmother let loose with a tree-rattling, "Kit—kit—kitty—cat—ACHOO!"

Before Grandmother could whisper "Bless my whiskers," Grizzorka captured her and tossed her into a deep black hole, chanting:

"Down you go,
and there you'll stay.
You should have known
to keep away."

ACHOO

And with a hideous cackle, she was gone.

Grandmother leaped and clawed,
trying to escape, but the hole
was much too deep.

"How will I save Tabithia when
I can't even save myself?"
Grandmother asked.

"Don't fret, Old Puss," replied
Spider, inching up the dirt wall.
"I have a plan."

Spider quickly set to work doing
what spiders do best. Before
long, she had spun an intricate
silver web. Not only was the
web beautiful, it was strong.
Grandmother grabbed hold of the
silken ladder and climbed up—up—
and out of the deep black hole.

Again, she crept toward the witch's hut and peeked inside. She saw Tabithia holding open a heavy cookbook titled *Goos, Brews, and Nasty Stews*. As Grizzorka added ingredients to her cauldron, a sad little "Meow" escaped Grandmother's lips.

Before she could whisper "Catnip and clover," Grizzorka captured her and locked her inside an iron cage, chanting:

"She was trapped in a pit and somehow got free. It won't happen again if she can't find the key."

Grizzorka hurled the key into a murky lake, where it sank out of sight. Grandmother rattled and clattered the bars, but she was locked up as tight as a secret.

"What now?" asked Frog, peeking out of her pocket.

"How will I save Tabithia when I can't even save myself?" Grandmother asked.

"Don't fret, Old Puss," replied Frog, squeezing between the bars.

He hopped toward the water's edge, and with a quiet splash, he dived into the muck on the bottom. He came up for air three times, and on the fourth try, Frog was carrying the key.

Grandmother unlocked the cage
and sneaked back toward the
witch's hut. She didn't see
Grizzorka or Tabithia, but she
did see Frog's brothers and
sisters huddled together,
waiting to be added to the
Halloween stew.

At the exact moment
Grandmother was freeing the
frogs, Grizzorka thundered
into the hut. Her hideous
screams sent frogs scuttling
this way and that.

Again, Grizzorka captured
Grandmother. She led her into
a deep black cave, chanting
with fury:

**"How Granny escapes
is a mystery to me.
But not from this tomb
will she ever break free!"**

Grizzorka's cackle caused a
huge boulder to crash down and
close off the cave's opening.
Trapped inside, Grandmother
pushed and shoved, but she
knew she'd never be able to
rescue Tabithia now.

"Tears?" asked Bat, slipping out of Grandmother's pocket.

"We're trapped tight this time," sniffled Grandmother. "The rock's too heavy, and I can't see in the dark. I might as well be blind."

"Don't fret, Old Puss," said Bat. "Blind's not bad for the likes of me. I'll use my radar to find a way out. Just stay close and follow my voice."

Bat led Grandmother through dark twisted tunnels until he discovered the back door of the cave.

Driven by love for Tabithia and heartened by the help of loyal friends, Grandmother marched straight back to Grizzorka's hut.

THUB, THUB, THUB-A-DUB, DUB!

She meant business and didn't care who knew it!

When Grizzorka spotted Grandmother and her brave army marching toward her, she chanted in anguish:

"I've battled a cat who has nine lives,
and she's only used up three.
Love for her kit runs deep and strong—
she's too great a match for me!"

Screaming through the woods, Grizzorka flew—never to be heard from again.

After a warm hug, Grandmother
hurried Tabithia home. They
arrived with just enough time
for Tabithia to slip into her
Halloween costume. And didn't
she look fine as she opened
the door to all the guests. She
greeted Spider, who brought
decorations, all fine and lacy.
She welcomed Frog, who
brought his family, all prepared
to make music. And she
welcomed Bat, who flew in with
an enormous tray of treats.

Grandmother, Tabithia, and
all their friends danced and sang
long into the night. Together,
they had turned a scary
Halloween showdown into a
fun-filled **Halloween hoedown**.

To Annie and Amy,
playmates and friends.
E.R.

To my longtime
friend and mentor,
Danny Kamerath.
L.R.R.

Text copyright © 1999 by Eileen Ross
Illustrations copyright © 1999 by Lynn Rowe Reed
All Rights Reserved
Printed in the United States of America
First Edition

Library of Congress Cataloging-in-Publication Data

Ross, Eileen, 1950—
The Halloween Showdown / by Eileen Ross;
illustrated by Lynn Rowe Reed. — 1st ed.   p. cm.

Summary: When Grizzorka the Witch snatches Tabithia
to be her new Halloween cat, Grandmother Katt dons a
pumpkin helmet and declares war, with the help of Spider,
Frog, and Bat.

ISBN 0-8234-1395-0

[1. Witches—Fiction. 2. Cats—Fiction. 3. Animals—Fiction.
4. Halloween—Fiction.] I. Reed, Lynn Rowe, ill. II. Title.

PZ7.R71965Hal 1999 [E]—dc21

98-12938 CIP AC

Design and typesetting: Yvette Lenhart